This book is dedicated to the two most influential Mothers in my lifetime. To my baby sister, Sandra Lynn– as a young, single mother you selflessly gave everything to ensure your son was happy, safe and always surrounded by people who had his best interests at heart. Because of you, he is a smart, kindhearted and spiritually grounded child. You have done an impeccable job and I am so proud of you for it!

My sister Sandra and her son Gunnar

And to you, Mom–thank you first and foremost for my life. Only now a Mother myself, am I able to appreciate the quality of person you have always been. You have been my mentor. I model my life after yours and am extremely proud to be your daughter. I love you, my treasured friend. I love you so much!

My Mom, Glenda and me

Acknowledgements

I have the utmost appreciation to Publish America for investing its trust in me. You were able to see my vision and provided me the opportunity to complete a goal. By doing so you have also given me the ability to teach my children that with faith and perseverance you can accomplish anything you set your mind to. I do truly thank you.

To my inner circle of close friends and family, without your encouragement I do not know that I could have crossed the finish line on this one. Just knowing you thought I was a writer with talent, had me believing that in fact, I was a talented writer. The power of suggestion is alive in all of us. Success is nothing if it cannot be enjoyed with those who mean the most to you. Thank you for all the years you have stayed involved in my life. I love you.

Mom, nobody but you will ever know the hours and hours that have been spent helping me on this project. Thank goodness you excelled in your English classes growing up because I did not! You also allowed me to share some very personal things about you, yet never questioned my intentions or my need to do so. As your child, I know that I still come first. Your knowledge and time have been invaluable to me. I will never find enough ways to express my appreciation for you, except to say this time I have the last word: I love you, MORE!

Most importantly I want to thank my husband and children for being the public sounding board for Mothers everywhere. I opened the door of our home for the world to see, and you graciously let me.

Children, your daddy and I might need a long vacation, but it's because of you that we might actually get one!

Finally Sweetheart, thank you for marrying me and blessing every day of my life in the most magical ways possible. I love you.

In the likely event I continue to write, I have chosen to use pseudonyms for our children: Amanda (age 4), Scotty (age 2) and Lindsay (age 1). Their new names were chosen after much thought and special consideration.

Table of Contents

www.lizmorehouse.com

Introduction

We all make choices that either work for us, or they don't. Sometimes the right decisions are also the hardest ones. I made the decision to become a stay-at-home mother. My husband and I felt that no matter what, our children would always have one of us home and that is exactly what we have done. While this sounds noble, and while it feels respectable, this choice to completely devote my life to family has turned out to be the hardest decision I have ever made! Somewhere along the way I got sacrificed. In attempting to be everything to everyone, I pushed myself out of line and mentally wandered off somewhere. The next thing I knew I was lost. I knew what made my husband happy and I knew what made my kids happy, but I forgot about the things that made me happy. It wasn't until I started writing again that I remembered.

Overwhelmed with my life and not wanting to be a burden on family and friends, I started to journal. I was already forgetting all of my hard work, the daily grind of being a Mom. I started sugar coating my life. I'd say things like *it's not that bad,* when sometimes it really was. Not wanting to imitate my mother, I began to diary this crazy life of mine so that some day I could prove to my kids exactly how hard I really worked for them!

After a few months of journaling the subject matters

changed. I started daydreaming about things I wanted to do again. One of the things I had forgotten all about was my love for boating. I had wanted a boat so badly. Some of my fondest childhood memories were of being out on the water. My husband was never introduced to that world and did not care about it as much as I did. Naturally, wanting a boat became a lower and lower priority to me. I had to wonder, was the only reason I do not have a boat today because I gave up on something important to me?

So here I am, knee deep in kids and smothered in bills. There was no way I could even think about getting myself that boat now. My daydream was suddenly further out to sea than ever before. However, just the thought of escaping to the dock seemed to ease my most difficult Mom days, so I kept entertaining the idea. Before I knew it, this daydream of mine became a goal. If I had thought convincing my husband was hard then, selling the idea now seemed impossible! But then I remembered something my mom taught me: *If I want something bad enough I can figure out how to make it work.* Just as that thought popped into my head, I was interrupted with the sounds of, "Mommy... Mommy!" Reality had re-entered the picture. Boat vs. bills. Common sense does not favor a boat.

Nonetheless, she was right and here I am trying to figure out how to get this boat of mine, that I intend to call the *Daydreamer*. I figured that if I was forgetting the hard Mom-stuff and selling myself short, you probably are too! I hope that my writing will make you laugh and

I hope it leaves you feeling inspired. But most of all I hope that you will remember the very most important thing you will ever give to your family is you! From the bottom of my heart I thank you again for reading my book. By doing so you have set sail to my dreams, Happy Mother's Day! Or whatever day today it is, enjoy!

~ Liz Morehouse

Communicating

I reveal an awful lot about my husband in this book and he's a sport for letting me do so. After all these years there is still only one thing that I would change about him. I wish he would like to dance. But that's it! That is all I would change. He is the perfect guy for me. I am more in love with him today than the day I discovered him.

He wrote something a while ago that still has me laughing every time I think about it and I thought the ending was the perfect way to begin my book. So in his own words let me introduce to you the person who has made my most important dreams come true, my husband, Jeff Morehouse.

In his own words

An important thing to realize when you're a Dad is that you aren't that smart. Most guys have an inflated impression of their inner genius and believe they possess the ability to understand even the most complex of problems if given the appropriate amount of time to think about it. When communicating with a child, the impression of one's self is like a shattered wine glass as it hits the floor.

Children arrive speaking their own language until we can convince them to speak ours. Unfortunately this process takes, well … I'll let you know when it happens. When they become confident in their ability to talk, you are in trouble. Babble, when used with enough English words, can somewhat resemble an actual sentence. However, resembling an actual sentence doesn't mean it is one.

In my household, *Mommy* and *Daddy* were a couple of the first words learned and understood. As cute as they sound coming out of your child's mouth, these words become the first tool they learn to utilize when it comes to getting something they want. What follows next is the babble sentence: *Daddy, I comd da util baf da ball.* This isn't an exact quote, as one thing you also have to realize is that you can't repeat the babble sentence. It is physically impossible. The child, however, cannot only repeat it verbatim, but also repeat it with conviction.

Once you, an intelligent, educated and *real world* tested veteran of life hear the conviction in the words, you realize that in fact, you are communicating. You then try and translate the babble sentence into your language in order to communicate back. The translation is the funny part. You can't do it without lots and lots of practice and even then it's dicey. In the beginning, what you think they say to you is probably nothing close to what they think they are saying to you. You will fire back something like, "You want me to get you the ball?"

"No Daddy, I comd da util baf da ball!" comes the

reply.

"Ohhh, you want me to turn the TV to baseball?"

"No Daddy, I comd da util baf da ball!" This time with more intensity.

At this point, you are thinking to yourself, "What the hell is he saying?" Not willing to quit so soon, you make a couple more attempts at responding to the child's thoughts before you finally realize that you have spent way too much time on this issue and are starting to feel that it's importance to has lost a lot. This is usually the time you just say, "Go see Mommy."

Simply Priceless

Motherhood is such an insane and crazy roller coaster ride. One minute you are thinking this child of yours is the most beautiful, precious thing life could offer, and the very next minute you might be cursing this little monster of yours for taking a permanent marker to the living room wall. Moments later, and with pride she says, "Look Mommy, pretty!" Instantly, well most of the time, you are back to being hopelessly in love!

All Moms get to experience Heaven's highest and most grand emotion, the love between Mother and child. There are so many kinds of Moms and so many kinds of kids. Overall, Mothers share an unspoken bond with other Mothers. Age does not matter, financial status, not even our religious backgrounds matter because in the end we know that we are meeting on common ground. Some days that ground might be quicksand, but it's *common* nonetheless.

Each of us can easily recall a time when our child has been absolutely, filthy-dirty from head to toe and what still comes to mind is how adorable they were! We might even have taken a picture.

All Moms have sat up suddenly in the middle of the night thinking their child is crying, or worse, scared.

Every one of us Mothers want for our children to love us and like us. We hate having to be the *bad guy*, but we do, to protect and teach our kids valuable lessons. As Mothers, there isn't one of us who have not endured overwhelming days where our kids are just too active or too hard to handle. We have all had those days where all it seems we can do is cry.

Some Moms can't cook, and some Moms can't clean. Maybe some of us don't know the answers to the homework assignments, or how to sew, or how to simply *just have fun*. Moms are not perfect, but we do have wings! Nobody can make a boo-boo feel better than a Mom. Nobody can hug and cuddle better than a Mom. And nobody can love you so completely with just one look the way your Mother can.

I wanted to be a Mother. I wanted to have children with the man I was in love with. I wanted to go to amusement parks and have Christmas mornings with my own children. I wanted to be more than an Auntie. The thing that I knew, but did not comprehend then, was that once you have children they are yours forever. What I did not understand was what forever felt like, at least not until I held my baby in my arms for the very first time. It's a powerful responsibility. Parenting is a lifetime commitment without vacations. Mini breaks, yes ... vacations, no. Of course, there comes a time that we'll have to let our children go, but that's because we love them! Moms never stop being Mothers though. We'll never give up worrying about them, we will never stop feeling the need to council them and we will never pass up an opportunity to brag about them with complete strangers. I know some people who have had their parents fail them miserably. I know parents who have caused unimaginable amounts of pain in the lives of their children. Personally, I know those people to be brave survivors determined to break the dysfunctional chain handed them. I know women who refuse to have their parent's behavior strangle and suffocate their spirit. It is those women who can make the best Mothers of all. I continue to find their stories helpful and inspiring on my most difficult *Mom-days*.

It just doesn't matter what your life was like before children because once you have them you cannot ever picture life without them. It's impossible to imagine them not ever being around. The first few months of Motherhood you'll begin reflecting, walking down memory lane–the one before kids. You start thinking of all the crazy fun and stupid things you did! Then you'll wonder, *Was this child in Heaven watching all this?* Then you'll ask yourself, *And this baby still wanted me to be their parent?* It's only then you start to appreciate how much this little child loves you, how much this child trusts you and how much this precious spirit wants to be with you.

Children open your eyes to a more beautiful world filled with bright colors and magical moments. With all that being said, it is hard to believe there are days where you wish you could go back where you wonder what life would have been like had you not had children. You wonder (at least once) what job opportunities, what possessions and what lifestyle might I be living if I skipped kids. Being a parent is hard and God knows, it's tiring. God also knows there are phases in your life when you forget about you.

I am learning that the most important thing in life I can teach my children is the ability to *remain true yourself*. It is going to be their strongest survival skill. It is their key to lifelong happiness. If my children can learn to remain true to themselves and learn to follow their dreams, then the bigger decisions they are bound to face in life will be made with confidence and much greater ease. While I realize this is the most important quality I can instill in my children, it is the hardest thing to teach them. The whole "do as I say, not as I do" is rarely effective. While I admit *being true to yourself* begins with me, I'm finding it nearly impossible to remember ME in this daily routine of tending to the needs of my family.

Since writing this book, I have discovered parts about myself that needed more care and more attention. Not just for myself, but for the harmony of my home and my family, too.

It's obvious that our world today continues to be seduced by power, prestige and money. It's everywhere you look. I know I am not alone when I say it's hard to dress up our *title*. We *are* just Moms. Everyone knows there's nothing glittery or glamorous about Mom stuff. Everyone knows we're surrounded by everything kid, and usually right down to the toilet seat cover! Everyone also knows that all the money in the world cannot duplicate or replace someone's Mother. We bring happiness into this world. We carry forward traditions into our families and our communities. As Mothers, we instinctively provide leadership and comfort to our own children, as well as every other child we come in contact with. As Mothers, we demand the means necessary to protect our children and every other child we may or may not know.

It does not matter what your life was like before kids, how popular you were or how smart you were. It does not matter how broke you were, how many struggles you had, or poor decisions you've made in your life. Your legacy begins the moment you commit to being a parent. From that day on, you can change however and whatever it is you want to be! In the eyes of our children, we are everything. In the eyes of our children, we can do anything. Our children cannot comprehend that we existed before they did. They will never believe that we really did have a life before we had them. So the moment we become parents, our slate is wiped clean. We have a brand new day to start over ... to reinvent ourselves. You know what that means, don't you? Along with getting a second chance at rewriting your own history, you have a second chance at dreaming brand-new dreams too. If we want to do it, I guarantee you ... our children will think we *can* do it! Being a Mother automatically means that we have a responsibility to bring love and beauty to this starving world of ours. Being a Mother means we become the foundation, stability and security of everything around us. Without Mothers our world could not survive. That means our world could not survive without YOU and I. We *are* simply priceless.

Still Small Voice

They say our lives really began with the birth of our first child.
Jeff and Amanda.

The biggest and brightest reward I've ever gotten, for following my heart's desire, is my daughter, Amanda!

Jeff is an only child and grew up in a relatively quiet home with his parents and two cats. Our house, on the other hand, had a revolving door because my parents liked to entertain. With a pool, a trampoline, a packed refrigerator and a ton of kids ... there was always something going on at our house!

When I first met Jeff, it was love at first sight. He had his head buried in some book, so all I could see was the top of his baseball hat. I never even saw his face. But literally my heart raced and chills went up and down my body the very moment I noticed him. I ran and told a co-worker that *I just walked by the guy I am going to marry!* He was doomed from the beginning. He had no idea that very day his life was going change forever! I loved him, whatever his name was.

It was nerve racking when we asked our parents to meet for the very first time. We were anxious, his family was hesitant and mine were happy just to have another occasion to celebrate! After the boating, the baseball games, the tailgating, the site seeing and of course the parties, his parents were ready to go back to where they came from! To say I made them nervous would probably be an understatement. I have been a whirlwind to his family since the day our worlds collided.

From the beginning it was plain to see that opposites had attracted. Jeff takes things in stride, and of course, with caution. Not me. I like taking things head on! So, as you can imagine the idea of children, not to mention having them, was a delicate subject for both of us. I wanted them. He did not.There have been many occasions in my life that I can recall being particularly intuitive. My children are living proof to one of those very predictions. From the start of our relationship I was insistent to Jeff, and anybody who would listen, that we were going to have three children. I sensed their personalities and even knew the order in which they would be born. I just knew it.

I had faith that Jeff eventually would warm up to the idea about kids, but he never really did. In fact, anytime I brought it up he would get particularly agitated. Unfortunately for us, kids remained the number one deal breaker in our relationship.

I tried for a while getting used to the idea that I was never going to be a Mother. I had myself pretty well convinced too. I plunged deeper into the Auntie role and it became a perfect distraction.

By now I had invested many years in our relationship and I was soulfully in love with him. I knew I could survive without him, I just didn't know if I wanted to. So, after many discouraging debates, I finally surrendered. I made a commitment about dropping the subject of children, forever.

But you know how that little voice works. It laid low for awhile, just long enough to make me think it was gone. Then it started all over hounding my thoughts even harder the next time around!

I am about to share with you something so private I doubt our closest friends even know this. But it is important. Three years into our marriage (and eight years all together), I told Jeff I could not follow through with it. I could not go my entire life without ever having kids of my own. I explained to him one last time that I had always believed there were three babies in Heaven waiting for us. I just knew it and I couldn't keep ignoring it.

Jeff could not have disagreed more. He got as irritated about this topic as he always had before and countered back boldly that he, "...NEVER wanted kids! Not ever. End of story."

I started to cry. I told him I could not change. I told him I had tried, but my heart would not let it go. He admitted to me that he too had been trying to change, but kept coming back to the fact he really just did not want to have kids and that he liked his life just the way it was. We talked all night and at the end of our conversation we came to a mutual decision ... to divorce. We loved each other so much that we knew we had to let go, it was only right. We even talked about our family and friends. How we would tell them, what we would say. We reflected back to our wedding day and highlighted some of our best times together. We talked into the early hours of the morning. It was a sad, sad night for both of us and we cried together many times. What happened you ask? Well, we did not divorce. We went a couple of days, letting it sink in. As far as I knew the chapter of my life with Jeff was coming to an end. It was confusing, too, because from the moment we locked eyes I could see our future together. There wasn't a doubt in my mind that the two of us were meant for each other. Not a single doubt.

Thank goodness for Guardian Angels because mine were busy working behind the scenes on Plan B! We hadn't said much to each other after that one night. We knew what was about to happen to us and it was really sad. But a few days later as I was making dinner he walked into the kitchen and said, "Okay, let's do it." My heart sank. I thought he was talking about the divorce and it was written all over my face. Heartbroken and scared, I just froze and started to cry some more.

Once he got that my sobbing was from the sad cry and not the happy cry, he grabbed me tight and quickly explained that we were talking about two different things! He had changed his mind after days of thoughtful prayer and meditation. He decided to hand his life over to God and trust He would take care of the situation. Jeff had never talked like that before … never.

As easily as I could have jumped at that offer, I did not. I feared he would end up resenting me. Tricking someone into getting pregnant is not love and I would never have done that to him. He was my best friend. I asked him to give it more thought, *just to make sure*. But as I said earlier, Jeff does not agree to anything he does not want to. Not even to me!

Nearly two years would pass before I became pregnant. But the experience of pregnancy was not joyful for either of us like you might imagine, after all that. I hated being pregnant and was having second thoughts about the whole thing. The entire nine months I had morning, noon and night sickness. But at the same time, I still could not stop eating thanks to some demanding cravings. Steak and mashed potatoes, to be specific. I had to have it! Also, mustard on a hot dog, but only for the mustard, mind you and the ice cream that followed! I was so emotional and even cried over toilet paper commercials. "That was the best commercial ever!" I'd blubber. Really! Yes, I was emotional.

Then there was Jeff ... he was freaking out too and did dumb guy stuff. He would say things like, "You're still hungry?" And, "So when this whole thing is over you're going to look like you did before, right?" And then there was his biggest concern, "Try not to have the baby on this date because there is an important race on." I mean he did dumb guy stuff! We made everyone around us crazy that entire year. We were weird and stupid until the end.

Then came the delivery. Oh man, that was entertaining for sure. In fact, we had nurses from other floors, other sections of the hospital flowing in and out of our room just to look at us. We'd made the hospital rumor mill. I'm guessing it went something like, "The couple having a baby in room 402 ... you've gotta take a look at them. It'll make you laugh!"

But you know what? Babies are magic! It does not matter who you are. The instant that little spirit enters the world, Heaven celebrates! We had been in the hospital almost sixteen hours when she finally decided to make her Grand Entrance. And Grand it was! She even had our doctor emotional, because she was suckling her (the doctor's) finger all the way through the birthing canal.When she popped out and the nurse put her to my chest like they do, Jeff leaned in and said, "Hi! I'm your daddy." I swear to you, at that moment she reached her tiny arms up at him and smiled. She did. You could have heard a pin drop! Everyone in the room was teary eyed, if not already totally balling their eyes out. I will never forget that. It was a beautiful, spiritual experience for everyone in that room.We did it and we did it right. However, little did we know the Angels were not celebrating because she was coming to us, but because she had left! Finally, Heaven found a couple that could handle her! A couple who tackles difficult situations with determination and humor. And my Angels no doubt, thought sending Amanda to Us, was humorous!

To this day, I imagine Angels coming from other departments saying, "Have you seen Amanda's family? Go look, it'll make you laugh!"

I am not just being a doting parent when I tell you our daughter's smile is contagious. She will command full attention in every room that she enters, whether you want her to or not! She does not care if she has to make a scene to do it either! She is a charismatic, intelligent, free spirited child without an ounce of shyness about her!

In a way, the day she was born, so was my husband. She woke up something inside him he still cannot put to words. He is different. My husband is a much more compassionate person. Before, strangers to him were just that, strange. Before, kids were a *pain in the ass* to him. Now, he dotes on every child who crosses his path. To him, every child is now cute or funny! He's changed so much that he will take notice of other people's kid pictures, intentionally. He even asks about them too. Jeff is a typical guy who lives and breaths sports. But now, if given the opportunity to brag about Fatherhood over baseball ... he will. He has gone from NEVER wanting kids, to wanting TEN! He loves, loves, loves little kids.

I have changed too. I thought I was unselfish, until I had a baby. I thought I knew about true love, until Amanda was born. I thought I knew everything there was to know about parenting, until I myself became a parent. I thought I worked hard, until I had children. I thought I understood devotion, until I became a Mother.

I have gambled everything before, and it is never an easy decision to make. Yet, every single time I do and every time I listen to my little voice, things work out just right. Not always like I think it's going to be, but always like it was meant to be.

I know Jeff loves me, because he loves ME! I will never wonder if we stayed together because I got pregnant. I will never *wonder* if I lived my life's purpose. I listened to my instincts and I know that I am living my life, *with* purpose.

MY life's purpose is to bring love into this world. My children exemplify hope, and happiness and love. Because of me, and because I stayed true to myself, good things have had a snowball effect. My still small voice was right, as usual. I am so glad I had the courage to listen.

Illusions

It's obvious kids change people. Before I had kids, I had standards for myself. They were high standards, but realistic standards. I was born into a large family and played the *mother hen* role. Having been around little kids my entire life, I was the best babysitter in the world. In fact, I had so many babysitting jobs that by age 13, I was practically naming my price. Later in life I was even a professional nanny. My resume for Motherhood had a wide range of qualifications and years of experience. Not to mention, we did not start *our* family until I was in my 30's, therefore I was *mature*, prepared and ready once I began my own venture into parenting. Or so I thought.

Having all of these natural instincts where children are concerned, it was obvious (at least to me) that my trademark in life would undoubtedly be *World's Greatest Mother*. In fact, up to and until the very day I found out I was pregnant ... I was convinced that Motherhood and me would make a brilliant combination! That was my first illusion.

I never thought that my kids would throw their food all over my walls and floors. I was going to teach my children manners and they were going to listen. Laughable now, I know. But remember, I write these illusions of mine, to help you. I share my illusions particularly for the women who think you know better than *us Moms*. I was one of you once. Trust me, I KNOW what I am talking about.

I never imagined that my most cherished sanctuary in the house was going to be the bathroom. It is, without question. Ask any Mother!

Nor did I think my kids would ever humiliate me in public, but they do. And never in a million years did I really believe MY child would have one of those screaming, flailing tantrums in the grocery store, like other Mothers endure! Not only has that happened to me, it has happened more than once. To add salt to the embarrassment wound, there was absolutely nothing I could do to change the behavior of my bratty child. That's right ... I said bratty child.

Another illusion: Kids are not always precious children with invisible wings. Kids also have invisible horns and really can be big brats! It took a while to admit this one. Because it sounds bad saying it out loud, but I swear to you, it's true. As I sit here this very moment writing, my baby girl is making my son cry! She keeps climbing on the couch to pull his hair. He's still waking up and just wants to watch morning cartoons. The baby is clearly enjoying herself, pulling his hair out. She is laughing and giggling with a mischievous and devilish attitude! She likes that he is crying and that she is the cause of it.

I never thought I would let my kids wear mismatched, stained or ugly clothes, but I do. And I could care less because they still look cute to me. However, let it be known–I draw the line when it comes to lint balls. Ugly … yes. Lint balls … no.

I never thought my house would be dirty. Not messy. Dirty. And I never thought my furniture would look like I frequented garage sales, but it does.

My microwave has all kinds of crusty explosions inside. Of course it's disgusting, and of course I notice. But I ignore it.

Speaking of disgusting, I never thought I would throw a plastic bag with a dirty diaper onto the back porch and let it sit for hours, before it made it to its final destination–the garbage can. But I have.

I knew that cleaning the gunk out of the corners of a highchair would suck. I just did not know how often you have to do it! Whenever I used to see a highchair with crusty noodles and soft brown bananas smeared all over, it was just proof to me that the Mother was a poor house cleaner. No, no, no! I know now that it was probably just a days' worth of food. I have since learned; most likely she figured if she cleaned the bananas after breakfast, she was going to have to clean the noodles out at dinner. I know now she was simply being time efficient with her daily chores.

I never thought I would allow my car to have crushed cheerios and toys covering the back seat, but you guessed it … it does. I did manage to take the stickers off the windows though; not easy!

I never thought having all the videos rewound could feel so invigorating.

I was never going to buy into the refrigerator art. Guess what? That's right, and I like it.

Don't feel too bad if this is happening to you also. I remember when I was stumbling over my own illusions because they were actually happening to me. The first couple of times I found it kind of funny. But then when it kept happening, I started to feel like a real snob! I realized I had been pretty judgmental towards the *other Mothers* and that maybe they did know something I didn't. Feel a little bad, because you should. But then simply call a friend, your sister, your mom and fess up to your illusions. You will feel better and they will feel GREAT!

More illusions...

I was never going to decorate my living room with a million pictures of my kids in different poses. Now? I do not have enough frames for all the pictures I want to display. In fact, I pretty much only have pictures of my kids in my living room. My kids were always going to have well groomed hair. They do, on special occasions.

I was going to be the kind of Mom who never raised my voice. I was going to be the kind of Mother who could reason with my child. Now? I have days, sometimes a cluster of them, where all I do it seems is yell or talk really loud. I have finally learned there is no reasoning with a child. I'm thinking that's what the word *child* means. You know when someone does not speak the same language as you, yet you try to have a conversation using a bunch of hand signals and are practically shouting? Of course, there's nothing wrong with their hearing, but you think by talking louder it will somehow translate. That is how I get with my kids. What's really dumb is that I know this and still catch myself doing it. That's particularly irritating to me.

I put my kids in front of the television so I can have a break, sometimes for hours. My mom did the same with me and Sesame Street. I turned out fine and learned the alphabet too. I let my kids run around in nothing but a diaper. It could be Winter, Spring, Summer or Fall. Around the time my first child hit two, I gave up trying to keep her dressed. Somehow by trying to keep clothes on her I just ended up doing twice as much laundry! I don't know how because she seemed perpetually naked, but it was true. The harder I tried, the more laundry I had. At some point I stopped trying. I finally accepted that kids just like to be naked. *Pick your battles* as they say; this is not one of mine. I have brushed my teeth after my toothbrush has been run down the wall (or worse) by one of the kids.

I never thought my kids would pour bath water onto the floor, night after night, after night. Why do they do this? They know I am going to get mad, but they do it anyway; they don't care.I never imagined I would have a *toilet kid*, but I do. My youngest child is our little fountain-splasher. It is pretty amazing how many different things she finds to put in there. We have a lock on the door, but with only one bathroom in the house and two currently potty training, she manages to slip in there … a lot! She's gotten sneaky too. She's figured out that shutting the door will buy her time. Sometimes I'm not really sure if the splashes are entirely fresh water. Once in a while someone undoubtedly forgets to flush! Like I said, I am potty-training two kids. Want to come over to my house or use the gas station bathroom down the street?

I have been in public with my child when they've had dried snot under their nose, or fresh snot smeared across their cheek. I see it, but sometimes I leave it for a while. I know that as soon as I clean it off, more will magically appear.

I clean the house before the teenage babysitter comes over. Why you ask? Because I don't want her thinking I don't know what I am doing. Stupid yes, but true.

I also make sure my house is spotless before I travel somewhere, so that if I die, I'm not caught with a messy house. Go ahead and laugh, but I know I'm not the only one! I've given my kids dessert for breakfast. I have bribed my kids to obey by rewarding them with a treat and I have broken the no-bottle rule just to get them to go to bed.

I have been known to swear in front of my kids. When they copy me, rather than saying that I was wrong I say,

Honey, you can't say that. Those are Daddy words.

I have dressed my bald, newborn baby girl in her brother's BLUE hand-me-down boy clothes. It just didn't seem to matter if everyone thought she was a boy. I eat cold food off of my kid's plate when they are finished. Glamorous, huh? I also lie to my kids about vegetables. I'll tell them, *Mommy loves this kind.* An illusion that works, so to me it's a *good lie.*

I thought my kids would always have a set bedtime schedule. Not babies, I'm talking about kids. That is a real joke. For any of you new Moms hear this, it's a myth. It's not true. Don't buy it! It's impossible. If someone's kid has always had the same bedtime and been happy about it … that friend of yours has been given a gift from the Night-time Gods. Either that, or they're flat out lying! Kids hate bedtime, all kids.

I say things like, "Because I said so and I mean it this time." or "I'll count, *1-2-3…*" Yes, I once had standards. I really did. They just changed. Lowered. Whatever!

I have finally surrendered to the fact that my kids will poop whenever they need to poop. Location is not a deciding factor for them. They do not care about the face-grunting process either. I do. But then, I happen to have constipation issues too.

I was in the store the other day and of course it was packed. I had all three kids with me and had been in line a long time. But I was determined to wait it out to purchase my items. During the wait, my child could not and created a big dump in their pants. A big, big poop. The kids were running around, not staying in line. They were bored. That of course only enhanced the odor. But I stood there tall, shoulders straight, my attitude pleasant and pretended I did not notice. I pretended it was not a big deal that my kids were getting unruly and I pretended the smell was not killing all of us. In fact, I just pretended there was no smell at all. I was attempting an illusion.

Though I admit it was a poor attempt, as everybody was looking around, mumbling to each other just trying to get me to say something. That used to drive me crazy when Moms did this! Oh, but now I know. And I do the same damn thing! I thought my lifestyle was not going to change much. I expected to keep eating at nice restaurants, just with well-behaved children accompanying me. I even thought I could travel on a plane without being the one with screaming, hyper kids. Illusions. I'm telling you, all illusions!

Have you ever been to a dinner party or business function and someone says, "I have to get home, my child isn't feeling well" or "We only have the babysitter for a little while." That was most likely an illusion, but a good illusion. My kids were going to be polite and quiet whenever I was on the telephone. Call me. See if that illusion panned out. You won't get through though. I keep the ringer off.

I *just knew* that when I laid down the law in the house my kids would listen. I really thought my children would take me seriously when I got mad. They don't care. Kids will do the time, just so they can do the crime!

Sometimes my kids pick their nose in public. It does not bother me, unless they wipe it on me (which is entirely possible). I'm not even going to address the bugger eating part, but let me just tell the delusional women out there... ALL kids eat buggers at least ONCE!

My kids have had *accidents* in the tub, in public and on my lap.

My kids have played in the cat box because they don't have a sand box.

My son climbs up on the kitchen counter, turns on the water, grabs the sprayer and hoses everything!

My daughter will climb on the bathroom counter to smear toothpaste all over the mirror. She also likes to decorate things with my nail polish.

They like going through my jewelry box, my make-up bag and my diaper bag. They like to band-aid everything. They like to change a gazillion times a day and they love unfolding the folded laundry!

My kids will stomp in puddles when they are clean, yank on animal tails and break toys on purpose. I don't know why, I just know they do. Childproofing is an illusion. It can sometimes be your illusion, rather than theirs. Kids are smart and can figure out any safety device you put in their way.

My daughter loves music and is constantly taking my clean pots and big spoons to play instruments. To the beginner Mom out there … this is a hassle for me because then I have to wash and disinfect all these dishes when she is done … and that could be five minutes later!

Though it's a near miracle to actually get them washed because my son (the love-every-button-kid) is always turning the knob on the dishwasher. If my dishes are drying, he turns the handle to wash. If the dishes are done, he starts it all over. He's my *helper*.

I had a completely different picture of what me with kids was going to look like. I talked a good game, but when the playoffs came (delivery) … I threw a Hail Mary and choked. I got a normal kid. The normal kid then turned me into a normal parent. For those of you without kids, understand one thing: I may sound like a slob with my messy kids, but kids are messy. You might see clean children around, but that's only because we decorate them up in public. And you might even see well-behaved children around, but that's because we are smart and only in public for a few hours at a time. It's planned that way. We are seasoned parents, we know better. It's an illusion… for you!

There is a saying, *the calm before the storm*. This is NOT an illusion. Newborns are the calm, after that it's all storm. Kids are stealthily quiet when they are about to destroy something, no matter the age. They are new little people wanting to touch and explore everything they possibly can. Kids have the most fun when they are making the most mess. Why do you think spaghetti is their favorite meal? Kids are simply a constant ball of motion, commotion, energy and activity.

I was a good babysitter because I came refreshed and only had to work a few hours. I got down on the floor and played with the kids. I was new and so they listened. I wasn't better. I was three hours with the little darlings vs. 2,000 hours. Then there was the nanny job; I only had to tend to the needs of the child ... ONE child. They had maids, a chef, errand-people and landscapers to do everything else.

You may disagree with some of my ways, but you're allowed and I don't really care. It's okay if you disagree with me or decide I could do a better job. Maybe you are right.

The wonderful thing about parenthood is that nothing else matters in life as much as your child. Parents do things different than other parents, but one thing is universal ... we love our kids more than we love ourselves! Everything we do is with them in mind. This is an exhausting job, an endless job and usually an underestimated job. We are bound to make mistakes.

If you are pregnant with your first child, you and/or your partner might notice strangers approaching you and talking to you as if you are family. They are welcoming you into the *parent club*. Soon, when your child is crawling, or walking and no longer willing to sit in the grocery cart or the stroller, you will begin to see exactly what it is you are in for!

Around that same time you'll begin wishing kids on people you know. That is normal and is actually an unspoken rule of the parent club. Dog people tend to be my personal favorite target, for *baby bomb wishes!*

If you are an overwhelmed Mother or Father, feeling like you are doing everything wrong, try not to be so hard on yourself. Your babies do not care if the laundry basket just dumped all over the floor. They just want to play in the empty basket.

Children are our teachers. The parenting process is similar to that of horse trainers where they must break the wild horse before it will accomplish the real stuff. To our children, *we* are the wild horses. If they have already broken you, stop crying and give them a hug. It's going to be all right. After all, Heaven hand-picked you to be their parent!

Illusions are okay. Illusions help you appreciate reality while at the same time resetting goals for yourself. I cannot explain it, but I am broke and my credit cards are nearly maxed. I have rolls on my hips to compliment my wide ass. I once had beautiful furniture and in a short period of time everything has been broken-repaired, colored on, stickered, stained and/or childproofed. I'm wearing sweats on Friday nights rather than mini-skirts. I know all the kid show characters and can speak their language too.

Life is not about possessions, but about the experiences. My child embarrassed me in public today and I stayed cool. That is a feeling of accomplishment that only a parent can appreciate. We get our pats on the back, parents, and when that happens it's an excellent feeling!

Like when my child says *thank you* to the bakery lady for the free cookie, or when my son wants to say his prayers without me bugging him. The very best moments are when one of my babies can calm a crying spell because they're looking eye to eye with me. These are rewards other people don't get. They are experiences, not things. And unlike things, it's the experiences that I get to keep forever.

That is NOT an illusion!

My Rainy Days

We live in the Northwest where it rains more times than doesn't. I happen to love this kind of weather and find it peaceful. A few years ago when my son was a newborn, we were having one of those typical stormy, rainy days. Except for the fact that my mood was stormy and my thoughts were anything but peaceful!

My mom was in town visiting so it didn't make much sense that I was in such a foul mood, but I was and it was obvious. In an attempt to turn the day around, she suggested we build a fire, rent some movies and have a healthy lunch. That seemed like a perfect idea until a few minutes into the movie the baby woke up crying. I was the only one to hear him, or so I thought. Naturally, I found this particularly annoying, as I was already in a bad mood. So I sat there for a minute and watched them, watching the movie. Finally Jeff said, "Do you want *me* to pause the movie so *you* can check on him?" Our son was having bouts of colic and we all knew I was the only one who was able to calm him. But it sounded different to me this time. It took nearly a half an hour, but I did get him settled down and quietly resting again. Rather than heading back into the living room, I went to the bathroom and drew myself a very hot bubble bath. Next thing I know I was crying. I couldn't stop and I didn't know why. What I did know, however, was that the more I cried, the madder I got. Mad that they were laughing and having fun without me. Mad at them for not noticing I was still gone. Mad at them because the baby was crying AGAIN! I was just mad at everything.

I finished my bubble bath, but had not finished feeling sorry for myself. I felt like I was going to explode inside; I was so emotional. I didn't even care that my clothes were sticking to me from having not dried off! I was frustrated, irritable and completely pissed at the world! I had to get away!

I did something I'd never done. I grabbed the keys and made an announcement, "The baby is crying!" Then I left, slamming the door behind me as hard as I could. I would be gone five long hours.

Like I said, it was cold and pouring rain, but as usual I was hot and had the air conditioner turned up full blast in the car! I drove to a nearby mini-mart and bought a phone card. With tears and mascara streaming down my face I made a number of phone calls. I called my two best friends and my sister, all of them Moms. Just my luck, no one was home! So I stood there, in the phone booth sobbing out loud and continued to call them. I just dialed and dialed for nearly an hour. Cars continued to pull in and out of the gas station. I was obviously distraught and people couldn't help but stare at me. I left rambling message after rambling message. I was complaining about my mom and complaining about Jeff. I gave up only when my phone card ran out. After that I got back in my car and began driving around, aimlessly. I did not know what to do or where to go. So, like any irrational woman I went to a *guy store* and purchased new windshield wipers. I was a complete bitch to the staff. I did not care either. I was a bitch on purpose.With my new wipers on, I continued to aimlessly drive around. It was very stormy. We were in the middle of a fierce, torrential downpour. I was sobbing and still pretty pissed. I should not have been on the road and I knew it too. I was driving recklessly. Weaving in and out of traffic, very impatient. But I didn't care.

I wound up wandering the mall in a complete daze. Again, people were staring. But I was in a confrontational mood. I didn't care about that either. Finally my aimlessness came to an end when I walked into a beauty shop. I treated myself to a facial; the first time in my life I had ever done that. I told the dermatologist that I was embarrassed with my face, as it was especially broken out. She was so kind. It was as if my Angels grabbed my hand and took me straight to her. Halfway through the massage I started crying again and could not stop. She left the room for a few minutes, so that I could gain my composure once more. I thought I'd been all cried out before I entered her shop. After a few minutes, she returned full of concern and compassion for me. She mentioned postpartum depression, stating she treated women like me pretty often. She explained my body was trying to get back to *normal*. Pregnancy being so intrusive to a woman's system, it can change our body chemistry dramatically. Often times it forgets how to correct itself once the baby has been born. This was not the first time I had been given this information, but it was the first time

I listened to it.

I left the salon feeling rejuvenated and peaceful, but emotionally drained. Finally I was ready to go back home. Jeff and my mom were relieved to see me walk in the door. Relieved that I was alive and unharmed. I had been gone all afternoon. They did not know what had set me off and did not even know I had taken a bath. When I had gotten up to take care of the baby, turns out they started making lunch for all of us and telling jokes. They were waiting for me to return and restart the movie. So, when I stormed through the living room and out of the house they were really confused! They told me a little while after I left, they began getting calls from the people I had called. I was too tired to explain and assured them I was okay, but desperately needed a nap.

Two hours later I came out of hibernation and saw that everything was running smoothly. The kids were playing with Daddy and Grandma. The kids had eaten, taken baths and the house was even clean. Right down to the kitchen sink!

Later that night I had a heart to heart talk with my mom. A talk *she* started. I was really uncomfortable at first and sat with my arms crossed, feeling very defensive. I have always been in control, so having had this unexpected melt down left me feeling vulnerable to failure.

Suddenly, I interrupted to argue my case listing all the reasons why I was a good Mom. Listing all the things

I did *right*. Of course, carrying on with the theme of the day, I cried some more! She just held my crossed arms and agreed with me, then finished my list for me. She listed the rest of the things *her little girl* had done right. Assuring me that my parenting skills weren't in question and that she too had been in my very shoes. She shared her *secret Mom confessions*. Things I never knew about her. Turns out she wanted to walk out some days too and she also had regrets once in a while.

Pregnancy happens every day, all over the world, but I had only done it two times. Moms have survived for years and they will continue to survive ... with or without sleep! We may feel average because women are pregnant all the time. And with the exception of loved ones, let's be frank here, we're not making the five o'clock news! But the honest truth of it is, we are creating life. We literally bless this world with miracles everyday! We are keeping hope and love alive. You and I! Moms have given the world George Washington, Jonas Salk and our beloved Walt Disney. It wasn't world leaders, but Mothers . . . WE did that!

I chose to be a Mother, but in all honesty I do not always want to be one. So whether it's depression, financial hardships, health problems, stress, fear or a broken heart you are experiencing, don't do it alone. You don't have to! Whether you are twenty-something, or your babies are twenty-something, if you are feeling overwhelmed please, please, please confide in someone! Don't wait until you reach the breaking point, like I did. I don't feel ashamed anymore that I want time to myself and I don't feel guilty if I can't do it all! This is a tough job, an exhausting job and an overwhelming job! Since that experience, I no longer see tending to my needs as selfish, but rather as responsible parenting on my part. Just because I am a Mom does not mean I have to forfeit my entire life. My wants and desires still matter to me as much they ever did. So ... If you can relate to the come-apart of my rainy day, but have not told anyone, will you?

If you know someone who resembles this situation, talk to them, would you?

If you see that lady in the store losing her patience with her child, say an Angel prayer for her. Toss her an understanding smile. Would you, please?

If you cross the path of a nice lady being particularly nasty (you know what I mean–intentionally bitchy!) be thankful you do not have her worries. Be understanding for those few minutes. Can you?

A smile. A hug. An encouraging word. Some humor. A bit of compassion goes a long, long ways for someone who is feeling tapped out. All Moms want to be good Moms, but some days we mess up. The forgiveness and understanding of others can be an enormous help. It's hard enough to forgive ourselves when we have a bad Mom day (or several of them). I was so thankful to that woman in the salon for taking me under her care and sharing with me her feelings. I am sure she has no idea that her compassion made such a difference in my life.

She probably thought she was just doing her job, just like my mom.

Love Notes

Jeff and I

For as long as I can remember I've gotten up at the crack of dawn with my husband as he gets ready for work.

Our routine has been the same for years. Most always I will make him a sack lunch. Only once in a while do I slack off and he has to eat out with all the other guys. You would think he would like that, but actually he prefers my soup and sandwich meals.

Growing up, my mom was a homemaker, like I am now. She was the neighborhood favorite, the *kool-aid Mom of Moms*. One of the great little Mom-things she did was to put love notes in our lunches and back packs. It took the sting out of being a brown-bag kid. I was always envious of the *punch card kids* who got to buy school lunches. I'd constantly beg and plead, "Please, please, can I have hot lunch today? Please Mom, please!"

It was the same Mom-answer every time, a resounding "NO." The only time we had hot lunches was on our birthdays. I was never seen standing in the cafeteria line with my friends, rather I was reserving the table for all of us. I'm not sure what was so appealing about getting a punch card. Maybe it was that the hairnet ladies, dressed in white hospital outfits, chatted with you as they ice-cream-scooped goop onto your orange tray or maybe it was the fact that you got a dessert every time. I'm not sure. Looking back, it was probably just the simple fact I wanted something I could not have. That is standard kid protocol. Right?

Anyway, my mom put notes in my sack lunches. I liked them and I looked for them. So did my friends. My mom got her love note reputation early on when I was in grade school and it followed her up into my high school years.

Her notes were famous, but I wasn't the only one anticipating them. I have vivid memories of classmates sitting around me asking, "Did you get one today?"or "What did she say?" Or they'd comment, "Her mom always puts love notes in her lunches" and "You're lucky!" I got stuff like that all the time and yet, being a brain fart of a kid, I still would rather have had the golden punch card.

Now here I am all grown up, on my own and continuing her legacy. Not to mention … surprise, surprise … I am no less popular for having been a sack lunch kid. Wouldn't you know, she was right about that too!

So as I was saying, for years I, too, have been writing love notes to my sweetheart on scrap pieces of paper. In fact, if I skip a few weeks, my husband will bring it to my attention. Which still surprises me because, like the brain fart kid I was, you wouldn't even know he got my notes. He'll only mention them when he's not getting them!

This morning was one of those days that I wrote him a quickie little love note. I even decorated it with colored markers. A little while later we did our usual *June Cleaver* thing and I walked him to the car. We shared our last kisses good-bye. I reminded him that he was tending the kids after work and *not to be late*. Then we teased one another about the kids. His last words were jabbing me about my bad breath! Then off to work he went.

As he waved one last goodbye, I thought about all the

years I have been keeping up my mother's love note traditions and that my honey was going to find another surprise from me today. In a euphoric state of mind, I walked back into the house smiling and loving *my guy* as I headed straight for the bathroom to brush my teeth, again! So far it had been a great start to what would undoubtedly be a busy day. I put my hair into my everyday ponytail and grabbed the toothpaste. Still zoned out, I leaned in towards the sink to scrub away, when all of a sudden I screamed! "AAAEEEWWW!" My love trance came to a screeching halt! Then I began repeating myself, "He's soooo gross! @%&#! He's soooo gross!" The sink was absolutely covered in long, dirty fingernail clippings! "He couldn't just turn the water on for two seconds and rinse this out?" I groaned.

Then suddenly seeing myself in the mirror, I had to laugh. I am so stupid. Here I am in this sick love trance, all romantic about my husband and pretending to be Mrs. Perfect Homemaker, when all the while I am sending my *six year old* off to work! Guys! He likes me to make his lunch, so he can show off that his woman does this for him! He likes love notes because it is attention. No matter what, husbands, boyfriends, athletes, movie stars, all of them are just dirty little boys, only taller! No doubt he drove off in his very own love trance. But his love trance was with the radio. Sports radio! And I'm certain that he too was in another world, only his world was calculating baseball scores and trades. I would bet that in his world and in his mind, he was worried how his team was doing. The *fantasy* team that he *coaches!* I'd also bet even money he was swearing at the dashboard, too. I finished brushing my teeth just long enough to get the toothpaste off the brush. I can't smell my bad breath anyway, so who cares? It's funny, the difference between boy brains and girl brains. Just when I think we are reading the same book, I turn the page and a pop-up picture appears!

Crap. Here we go again. The kids are awake. *Mommy*

... Mom. Whaaaaa! All in a matter of 30 seconds too. Amazing. Oh, the romance. You have to love it!

I Need Mommy

"Mom, I'll get it. Mom, I'll do it. Mom, I'll fix it. Mom, Mom, Mom!"

It's been five long years since I have actually cashed a paycheck. Yet, I have to tell you this is the longest run at a full-time job I have ever had! I was one of those employees who easily got bored and had a tendency to move on. This Mom-job does not afford that luxury. I don't mind the job. It's the no-salary that I mind. I miss being able to stay up late if I want. No matter the day, my kids are up before the birds chirp. Instinctively I play defense and am always going to bed early, always. I don't mind. It's not being able to sleep three consecutive hours that I mind.

I don't mind tripping over safety gates. I don't mind tripping over toys. It's shoving my toe into the wall afterwards that I mind.

I don't mind stopping mid-meal to help my children, nor do I mind sharing my food with them. It's the kid backwash that I mind.

I don't mind making my husband something to eat just as I'm winding my day down; of course I don't offer either. I don't mind making something different for every single person in the house for that matter. It's when they don't touch it that I mind.

I know that no matter what, someone will always discover me hiding in the bathroom! It's when they are flushing the toilet (with me on it), trying to peek behind my butt and shredding the toilet paper for me that I mind.

I don't mind running to the store for ANOTHER gallon of milk. It's paying for it that I mind.

I don't mind that a little person always has to sit on my lap or clamp onto my leg. It's when I take ten steps without them and they cry that I mind.I don't mind being the bugger collector and I don't mind being farted on. I don't mind wiping drool, or being drooled on. It's being buggered-on that I mind.

I don't mind running the dishwasher twice a day. But having to hand-dry all the mismatched plastic cups and spill proof lids I've acquired over the last few years that I mind.

I don't care that when I take out the garbage I'm going to get the smell of dirty diapers in my face as I shut the lid. It's changing all the *stinky* diapers that I mind.

I don't care that my kids are fighting in the background when I am on the phone with a creditor or making doctors appointments. It's when I'm trying to talk to a friend that I mind.

I don't mind being the bad guy in order to get the tangles out. It's the crocodile tears that I mind. It kills me. But then I remember my mom doing it to me when I was a kid and then I don't mind all over again. *Hold still honey, I'm almost done.*

I don't mind constantly performing the Heimlich on my kids because they've eaten too fast. It's collecting the mashed food in my hand that I mind.

I don't mind not having anything new in my closet to wear and I don't mind sporting the grunge-look at 35 either. It's when I am at the grocery store looking down at my list and realize there is a big stain on the front of my shirt that I mind! Yeah really, that's the only time I mind.

I don't care that the kids are destroying something new. Whether it's yanking the flower tops off in my garden, or ripping the pages out of yet another book. I might yell at them for it, but I have to. Otherwise, I really don't mind. It's just stuff.

I don't mind seeing little handprints on EVERYTHING from the windows to the TV! It's when they are doing it behind me as I clean that I mind.

The last thing I don't mind about Motherhood is being last. Last to eat, last in line, last to get waited on, last to get pampered and without a doubt, the last to get into bed. I don't mind being last anymore.

None of this stuff bugs me. It just bugs me when it happens all the time! The thing I have learned about being a Mom is, we don't mind. We expect it even. In fact, we like being the go-to guy.

It's just that this Mom stuff feels really lonely sometimes. You know what it is like. By the time the dust settles you are so exhausted that if you do have a moment to send a letter to a friend or treat yourself with a manicure, it just seems like one more chore that needs to be done.

I know kids must have this consistent, mind-numbing structure. I realize that by providing this day in and day out it's making me a good Mother. But some days I just wish it were a little different. Not a lot, just a little. I wish I could enjoy a hot shower and not know someone was breaking into the snack cupboard. I wish I had the option to sleep in. I wish that I could vacuum and not pick up crushed cereal five minutes later. While I'm at it, I wish I didn't have to repeat myself every few minutes.

I know that someday all this will be gone and someday my house will be clean. I know that the noise will not always be at ear-piercing levels, but I also know I won't have a baby to cuddle with either. I love my life and the monotony of it all, so I guess the only thing I would really change about my job is the pay. The pay sucks! That I mind!

Is The Grass Really Greener?

Last week a friend passed away. Like most deaths I imagine, it was shocking and unexpected. In my lifetime, I haven't known many people who have died. This was especially unexpected, to me anyway, because this friend committed suicide. This friend of mine was a larger than life storyteller and really appreciated a good joke! To me that is what made his death so ironic. Not a very funny punch line, for a funny guy.

The morning the phone call came, death was the furthest thing from my mind. The sun was shining and the birds were chirping; they really were. It was so perfect actually that the kids and I were enjoying breakfast on the front porch before heading to the park. But once I got that phone call, the rest of the day took a dramatic turn. The first thing I did was to lower my flag to half-staff. I then began to make the necessary travel arrangements to attend his funeral. I was in a state of shock. I started to do things that made little or no sense. All I wanted to do was hand-wash dishes and shave my legs. Two things I hate doing and two things that are always on the bottom of my to-do list. But that's what I did. I washed every dish I could get my hands on and I shaved everything in need of shaving!

Then I proceeded to get drunk. I drank and cried into

the wee hours of the morning. I had barely three hours of sleep before it was time to get up and leave for the airport and I still had not packed. I knew I was in for a miserable day when I was taking a shower. I kept forgetting if I had washed my hair. Plus I had the spins something fierce. I definitely had one hell of a hangover! I couldn't remember how much wine had been in the box; it could have been a whole box for all I knew. I know it felt like it! I had punished my body and it was giving me a fierce payback. I had hot and cold sweats, nausea, vomiting, a splitting headache and puffy, glossy eyes. I was a mess! My shuttle service arrived as I was leaning over the toilet hurling my guts out. I was trying to strike a deal with the Porcelain Gods. I begged, "Please let me keep the medicine down long enough for it to work. Please!" No such luck. I answered the door with a cold washcloth to my face. It was 4:00 a.m. Fun times.

Once on the plane and in the air, I began thinking about the sadness of it all. It was hard to believe that I was traveling to attend a funeral for someone I loved. I tried to imagine what it was like to feel as desperate as he must have felt. Then I remembered that in fact, I had. Only once and it was years ago, right before my parents divorced. For a fleeting moment I too had considered suicide. Attempted it, in fact. I was driving home from a family counseling session. Furious and emotional, I swerved off a freeway exit. I accelerated my speed and steered towards a cliff, but I turned away at the last second. Skid marks scarred the road.

That was a big moment in my life. I could have ended

it, but my little voice inside reasoned with me. So I wondered, *Where was my friend's little voice? Did he hear it? Did he ignore it? What the hell happened?* I stared out the window, 30,000 miles in the sky, watching the clouds floating below. *Where is he?* I asked. I looked down at my three month-old baby and my tears trickled onto her face. I could not imagine missing all this. My life has been filled with experiences that I would not trade for anything, not even the bad ones. I felt very sad for him and for his family. He was a Dad too. That is what was really made it unbelievable to me.

I arrived at my destination and I met up with mutual friends at a local hotel as we planned to attend his funeral together. The support was good and allowed for the sharing of memories and comfortable laughter in honor of our friend.

I was nervous to see everyone, being a new Mom and all. I felt fat and my clothes were out of style. So not wanting to feel out of place, I went shopping for a new funeral-outfit. I even had my girlfriend color my hair. I know now this sounds really lame, but at the time it made perfect sense! It wasn't until I got home and the shock had tapered off, that I realized no matter how I would have shown up, I was still looking better than the guest of honor! We all were. *Fat? What rolls? Zits? Where? Run in my nylons? Didn't notice.* Funerals just create a strange sensation all the way around.

I know his wife was pretty mad at him for checking out early and dumping all his problems onto her lap. His final wish was to be cremated. She honored that part for him! Before the funeral services a few of us had gone to visit *his spot* and privately pay our respects.

I could not help but notice the location looked vaguely familiar. Something reminiscent of the television show *Cops*. Driving the few miles leading into the cemetery we saw nothing but brown lawns, torn couches and weight sets parked on front porches. Dogs were chained and circling trees, instead of their tails. There were guys everywhere walking around shirtless, carrying brown paper sacks. I thought, *She must be really pissed to put him here.* In fact, I think it's worth noting, the box she chose was at the very top of the wall, as if to make him look at this creepy wonderland for eternity! Under the circumstances, it seemed she'd chosen a most fitting *time-out*.

Funerals get thrown together so quickly. It's not like planning a holiday party or a summer vacation. For that very reason funerals are hard to get off the ground without a hitch. *No pun intended.* The services were held at his church. Afterwards, dinner was served for his immediate family and close friends. Lasagna. Yummy. Reminded me of the gross song we used to sing as kids, *The worms crawl in, the worms crawl out ....* Might as well have served spaghetti. You could tell the ladies from his congregation organized the meal because it was typical of his church socials! We had paper plates to match the paper cups. There weren't even pictures on the paper towel napkins; just plain white. I guess it coordinated best with the butcher paper tablecloth. Besides the lasagna and water, we had ambrosia salad, jello and lots of cookies, brownies, and sweets. A real carbohydrate-heaven send off! My friend would have loved it!

We stayed late visiting with other out of town guests. The tables and chairs were being broken down and the tablecloths ripped off. Another party was being set up … a wedding party in fact. The world just keeps going round and round. As we watched the people bringing trays of food into the church it looked a lot different than our feast. They had platters of big juicy strawberries, decorative watermelon baskets, a pretty crystal punch bowl, sprinkled pastel mints and a three-tier cake with flowers on it. I thought, *Man, the difference between life and death!*

This past week was a fairly emotional one for me. While I believe in life after death, the enormity of it all is still hard to grasp. I will say that the hours traveling home allowed for a chance to review my own life. My friend's death gave me a greater appreciation for having conquered struggles in my own life. It also gave me a greater understanding for how difficult circumstances really can get. I considered all the things I would have traded if had bowed out early like my friend. I wondered what he had traded for his decision.

I renewed goals and dreams for myself on the long ride home. My friend's death reminded me how I've taken things for granted, like enjoying sunrises and spending time in the mountains. I thought about all the things I wanted to teach my children. I thought about all the things I wanted to share with my husband. I had forgotten about how many things I really wanted to do. At the risk of sounding insensitive, I found my friend's death therapeutic. It felt so good and peaceful holding my baby, Lindsay. It felt good tending to my looks for the week. It felt good visiting with friends and laughing. I felt good. Now it was time to go home.

After an entire day of being in cars and airports, I did just that. As the shuttle driver pulled up to my house the first thing I noticed was that our flag was still flying at half-staff. My *funeral vacation* was officially over. On the front porch stood my son, screaming at the top of his lungs and in a very soggy diaper. Next to him, stood my drama queen daughter in all her glory, wearing one of my fancy nightgowns, dress up shoes and of course, a crown. The most glorious sight to see though was my husband, looking like I do after a day with them!

Maybe it wasn't quite the romantic scene I had conjured up in my head minutes earlier, but it was all mine! The very last thing I thought as I walked back into my hectic home was, *The grass is always greener ... unless of course, you are at John Doe's funeral home!*

Rules, Rules, Rules

There was nothing particularly special about yesterday. I had doctors appointments, laundry, dishes, kisses and time-outs. My husband wanted tacos for dinner and had been calling from work since 11 a.m. to make sure the meat was thawing and that I was getting everything ready for when he walked in the door. He came home at the usual time but holding a bag of accessories for *his* taco. I had just started to shred the cheese and the microwave was thawing the meat. In fact, I was punching the defrost button and wiping sweaty hair out of my face, from chasing the kids all day, as he pulled up to the house. His first words were, "It's not ready yet?" I just looked at him like he was an idiot. He changed out of his work clothes and came back into the kitchen. Not to help, oh no. To lean against the counter and watch me get *his* dinner ready.

The kids were racing in and out of the kitchen stealing shredded cheese and running back outside, their voices piercing my head with high pitch shrills like a pack of mischievous hyenas. He started to read me this thing he got at work, but quickly got frustrated because I was not listening. My brain was multi-tasking to its limit. He yells, "Hey, outside! I'm trying to talk to your mother!" Then he turns back to me and continues, "Okay, listen to this thing this guy at work sent me. I sent it to your mom. She thought it was REALLY funny."

I said, "Good. I could use something funny." He proceeded to read me this list making sure I knew they were all listed #1 on purpose.

The message in the email reads, *I know I will get in trouble for passing this on, but it's funny.*

Subject: The Man's Side of the Story (author unknown)

Finally! The Guy's side of the story. We always hear *the rules* from the female side. Now here are the rules from the male side. These are our rules! Please note that these are all numbered #1 ON PURPOSE!
1. Learn to work the toilet seat. You're a big girl. If it's up, put it down. We need it up. You need it down. You don't hear us complaining about you leaving it down.
1. Sunday = sports. It's like the full moon or the changing of the tides. Let it be.
1. Shopping is not a sport. And no, we are never going to think of it that way.
1. Crying is black mail.
1. Ask for what you want. Let us be clear on this one: Subtle hints do not work! Strong hints do not work. Obvious hints do not work! Just say it!
1. *Yes* and *No* are perfectly acceptable answers to almost every question.
1. Come to us with a problem only if you want help solving it. That's what we do. Sympathy is

what your girlfriends are for.

1. A headache that lasts for 17 months is a problem. See a doctor.

1. Anything we said six months ago is inadmissible in an argument. In fact, all comments become null and void after seven days.

1. If you won't dress like the Victoria Secret girls, don't expect us to act like soap opera guys.

1. If you think you're fat, you probably are. Don't ask us.

1. If something we said could be interpreted two ways, and one of the ways makes you sad or angry… we meant the other one.

1. You can either ask us to do something or tell us how you want it done. Not both. If you already know best how to do it, just do it yourself.

1. Whenever possible, please say whatever you have to say during commercials.

1. Christopher Columbus did not need directions and neither do we.

1. All men see in only 16 colors, like windows default settings. Peach, for example, is a fruit, not a color. Pumpkin is also a fruit. We have no idea what mauve is.

1. If it itches … it will be scratched. We do that.

1. If we ask what is wrong and you say "nothing," then we will act like nothing's wrong. We know you are lying, but it is just not worth the hassle.

1. If you ask a question you don't want an answer to, expect an answer you don't want to hear.

1. When we have to go somewhere, absolutely anything you wear is fine … really.

1. Don't ask us what we're thinking about unless you are prepared to discuss such topics as baseball, the shotgun formation or monster trucks.
1. You have enough clothes.
1. You have too many shoes.
1. I am in shape. Round is a shape.
1. Thank you for reading this. Yes, I know I have to sleep on the couch tonight, but did you know men really don't mind that? It's like camping.

"Pretty clever, huh? Some of them really funny, huh?" I was laughing, but what made me really laugh was that, as my husband got further down the list his tone of voice changed. He was no longer just telling jokes, but it was like *he* was telling *me*. It was like someone gave him the rule list and he was laying them down like the powerful patriarch he envisions himself to be. I just listened, as I continued to make his dinner and chase the kids out of the kitchen every 30-seconds. By the time he was finished, I knew the damn list was going in my book.

I had zoned-out thinking about all the hundreds, maybe even millions of guys who were getting this *rules list* via e-mail today, or next week. In my pea-brained head, I was calculating all the wives and girlfriends like me having this same experience. Then he gets to the end of his list. Chest out, he's not finished. He tells me about the guy having to sleep on the couch, like he was some hero; some martyr for him and all the rest of the poor guys having to endure this life they sometimes call "hell."

Please. I just laughed. Not with him, like he thought,

but at him! I thought, *I've got some rules for you too!* But I did not have time. I was STILL trying to get *his* dinner made. I chased the kids outside with the knife in my hand, waving it around as I called at the kids, *Hey! I said outside!* This time I followed them out to the porch. They took off like little mice, running down the stairs to the grass, yanking the laundry off the clips as they sped off. This time I got mad. Past tolerant, past frustrated. I got mad. I went back inside and said, *These kids have been like this all day. They are just crazy.* Then I said, *Oh yeah, did you see what I did today? Look outside.*

He looked. He searched. Never mind that it was right in front of him big as life. He kept looking. Right as he was about to say, "What?" he saw it and covered his eyes to keep the tears in, the tears of laughter. He was laughing hysterically. I said, "What? I thought it was a good idea. Of course, the kids have been ripping the clothes off all day, and the weather is cold so the clothes are not drying, but ..."

He replied, "You should have seen that coming."

I countered, "But the dryer is just so loud! I could not stand it anymore!"

See, we bought this house a year and a half ago. First-time homeowners; built in 1925, a *fixer-upper*. When we were in negotiations, I vividly remember our real estate lady coming to our apartment to sit with Jeff and me as she went over the binder list of things the inspection had found. Jeff sat there, being Mr. Impressive with comments like, "Oh I can fix that. I can rewire that. That just sounds big; it's not really. I can repair that easily." By the end of her notes, we decided it was do-able.

My husband is really intelligent and he does know how to fix all that stuff. *Doing it has been another deal!* Let me tell you how he explains it to me and see if it sounds vaguely familiar to any of you. "I worked all day," he begins. "The traffic was HELL! I get so tired from working and commuting on top of it. I'll do it this weekend. I just need to unwind and watch the game." (Any game. It does not matter what sport, just the game.) The weekend comes. "Babe, I know I said I would get to it, but I am just so exhausted. I'll tell you what. Let me just relax today, watch the game and I will do it tomorrow." Tomorrow comes, "Hey Babe, I know I said tomorrow, but this weekend has flown. Besides the race is on and I wanted to drink some beer. Tomorrow is Monday already. Can I just watch the race? Next weekend. Promise." Then for the times I get real frustrated he throws in, "I fix things all day at work. That's a big job. I'll have to go all the way up to the (fill-in-the-blank specialty) store. By the time I get home I won't be able to fix it tonight anyway." You know the ending to this story. I fix all the stuff I can, live with what I can't and hire help for the things I have to get fixed.

So anyway, back to today. We have this dryer. It is on its last leg. Maybe that's why it shakes so violently. This thing is dying a slow, painful death. You can hear it down the block. It is in the basement and when it is running my upstairs floor vibrates. Yes, it can still dry stuff. The stuff it does not eat, that is. The back of the vent thing has been duct taped to death. Yet, everything within a five-foot radius still has lint on it. My husband hates the noise so much, I can't run it at night. He can't *concentrate on the game.* I cannot run it at naptime, or early morning either. The kids can't sleep if I do. Besides, it is rude to our neighbors on either side of us. So, today I got sick of it. I went down to my husband's toolbox and found yards and yards of electrical wire. Wire that is cut on both ends; wires without plugs. See, he knows how to fix stuff, so he collects stuff; things he could "use."

I took the wire and hooked one end around my neighbor's fence, circled it around our back porch and tied the ends together in big fat knots. And waa-la! I had made a homemade laundry line! I even had a bunch of clothes clips in my kids' craft stuff. The problem was the kids thought it was fun to re-clip my clothes and yank off the other ones. They ran in circles around the deck. They had me outnumbered as I chased them. The clothes were not that clean anyways because our washer also sucks. But now I was back at square one. The clothes that had not fallen on the ground now had sticky-kid handprints on them.

Jeff said to the monsters (kids ... whatever), "Hey don't do that. Your mom worked hard on that." Then he came inside with a handful of something and says, "Okay new rule! Your underwear does not go up! None of it! I don't care. Your underwear cannot go up!"

I looked at him, knowing he was serious. Picture this.

I'm sweaty all day from the housework and kids. I hardly wear make-up anymore and I am fat from being pregnant three years in a row. But yeah, at times he's still a jealous boyfriend! Guess he does not want the elderly men in the neighborhood looking at my dingy bras and size huge underwear.

I'll admit, for a millisecond I was flattered. Then I went back out to round up the kids and bring them inside. I really needed to finish dinner. However, then I noticed Jeff had managed to grab my underwear, but left the other clothes on the ground. I lost it right then and there! I'll admit it. At that point I had a temper tantrum! I grabbed the laundry basket and started muttering and yelling at the same time. Then I yanked off everything that had been left on the line and threw it all in the basket. Impatiently I cut off my makeshift clothesline wire things so the kids would not accidentally hang themselves playing a game. *Why do I even try?* I thought to myself.

Then I heard Jeff saying, "Kids, let's leave Mommy alone. You made her mad." He was being real sweet to them. URRRGHHH! Rules, rules, rules! I've got some rules!

He came and took the knife out of my hand and said, "Honey, I don't think you should have that right now." Wisely, he found a cutting board and started helping with dinner. I calmed down and we finally ate. In fact, he and I ate outside on the deck (he never wants to do that). He put the kids in the bedroom and said they could eat later. Of course, they stared at us the whole time and knocked on the window making faces, but we ate and read the newspaper and tried to relax together. It was nice. Once in a while we laughed, both for different reasons I am sure. The next morning he told me to go buy a brand new washer and dryer. He insisted it was okay to charge another $600 to one of the cards. I worried, then thought of the alternative. It's stupid really. Getting excited about going into deeper debt all for the purpose of doing more chores.

It's this sort of stuff that makes me think about sex-ed classes and teenagers. They do not need to worry themselves with bananas and condoms. They should still call it sex-ed, but start the year with a couple experiencing pregnancy together. Vomiting, mood swings, weight gain and more mood swings. Of course, the delivery … film for that! Scare the hell out of the girls. Gross out all the boys! Be sure to show the after birth! Then in the middle of the school year, go through the basics of a relationship. You know … the communication courses. Then the end of the year you teach them about debt, kids and the so-called pleasures of adulthood with the accompanying responsibilities. You know, *real* Sex-Education! Rules. Nice try.

By the way, I did leave the house the very next morning with the three little Angels, all clearly in need of a tubby, a hairbrush and manners. (I don't have a car, so we stroller everywhere.) But what the heck, I was going to pick out a new washer and dryer! I don't know exactly why I still am irritated with that rules list. I mean, it was funny. Maybe it was the delivery of the list. Maybe it was the fact that the author and my husband were actually serious. Maybe it was that they were all listed #1! I'm not sure and don't really care either. I just wanted every woman, girlfriend and wife out there who are either married, dating, or sleeping with someone like *My Guy* to know that when I did leave the store today after purchasing my brand new washer and dryer set, I had also bought myself a beautiful new dishwasher! I also made sure the delivery guys are taking away my old stuff. You cannot return the new dishwasher if the old one disappeared, can you?

Rules. You have to love it when the man starts thinking he's wearing the pants. Have a nice day out there friends and remember, like I always say to my husband, "Just because you watch sports all day does not make you an athlete!"

DO OVER

You know, today sucked! Today started off bad and kept on getting worse! I could not catch a single stinkin' break. It was one thing after another.

It all started about 3:30 a.m. My son woke up crying because his bed was soaked. I changed his diaper and his sheets and put him in a clean pair of pajamas. Then finally, I kissed him back to sleep.

My eyes were so tired ... the best I could do was squint my way through the Mom-stuff. I was pretty much on autopilot. As I turned the light back down, my baby woke up. So, I made a fresh bottle and changed her too.

After what seemed like an hour later, I climbed back into my bed. Only now I have to push, lift and roll my three-year olds sleepy, deadweight body off my side and off my covers. It's always a challenge too, because my husband undoubtedly has gone diagonal! It's amazing that he *never* seems to hear the kids in the night and has no idea of how many times I am up with them. Yet, even in his comatose state of mind, he'll know exactly when to go spread eagle across the entire bed!

What really sucked was that when I pushed my daughter to the middle I discovered that underneath her, on my edge (side) of the bed was an enormous wet spot!

Round three. I changed her bottoms and put her into some clean pajamas. Then I quick-fixed the situation with a couple of dry towels. No wonder I have so much laundry to do.

Not to mention, I do not even remember her climbing into bed with us! I would like just one night where my bed belonged to me again.

Now it really has been an hour and my day starts in a mere thirty minutes. I gave up and got up. It was 4:30 a.m. Nobody noticed I was gone anyway. Maybe I could get some quiet time.

Well you know how it is, that fantasy shattered fast when the baby heard me breathing. *Mommy's awake?* Instantly she wanted to play! My day had officially begun. So with my happy face on, I picked her up out of the crib. I confess she was pretty cute, all bright eyed and bushy tailed, kicking her back legs in glee.

Over the next two hours the other munchkins wandered out of bed. One thing that really irritates me though is when they wake up grouchy, crying and demanding things all before I have even had a chance to tend to their normal needs. It takes me back to my days as a nanny, where I was expected to cater to everyone and appreciate doing so. The only difference between then and now is that the pay is considerably less and I don't get to travel!

So here we are at mid-morning, but I've already punched seven hours on the time clock and still no break. It's Fall, so naturally it's too cold for a stroller ride and too cold to play outside since they are still so little. My kids are rambunctious and have been showing signs of cabin fever for days.

They are getting into everything that's off limits. Breaking into the kitchen cupboards, throwing clothes out all over the floor from the closets I just organized and they are chasing and tormenting the poor cats. They aren't interested in television and they don't want to play with their toys. Their only mission today: search and destroy!

I thought if I took a shower I might feel better. Wrong! In that short time my kids got into the refrigerator and took chunky bites out of butter cubes, poured the milk out and took turns cracking the eggs! Then they streamed a brand new roll of toilet paper from room to room. And it was our last roll; I had to *fix it.*

After their time out, I grabbed the craft box in a vain attempt to change the mood of the day around. But the kids just put the stickers on furniture and argued over the markers … markers they were not even using.

My neighbor called and asked me to baby-sit her child because she was in a jam. I *graciously* agreed. Why did I do that? Another kid, just what I was praying for (Dyslexic Angels … you gotta love them!).

My son started up a game of baseball in the living room and knocked over one of my houseplants; dirt went everywhere. I had just left the area for a minute to grab *another* load of laundry.

Someone poured all the dry cat food into the water bowl and made a big sponge mess!

Recently we took in a stray cat. She is nervous and will not use the liter box. She keeps pooping, and peeing around the house. But today, it was on my bed ... my side of the bed to be specific. I know she's trying to tell us she's having a hard time, but I knew that already. She could have urinated on Jeff's side! I still would have ended up washing all the blankets, but I would have appreciated her going to someone else for help; someone other than me. At least today anyway; it's barely one o'clock!

One of the potty training kids had to go. But rather than using the toilet, she thought it would be interesting to see what happens when you do it standing up, like boys do. Meanwhile the copycat sibling, pooped. Only he decided it would be fun to smash the pellets down the bathroom sink! I can hear them now: "Watch, Sis."

"Oh, good idea, Scotty." They have always been great teammates.

I was feeding the baby at the time and they were quiet. I was trying to catch my breath.

After I bleached up the bathroom *accidents*, I marched Thing One and Thing Two to bed. On my way out of their room I stepped in cat poop, the second feline protest of the day. I told you this day sucked! None of this is made up either. This is an actual day in my life!

I was in the middle of about 50 loads of laundry when my husband called to see "how my day was going." A phone call he surely regretted making. As soon as he asked, I went on a five-minute rant about *his* children and *his* cats, all without taking a single breath!

His only words to me were, "You are so lucky to be at home."

Oh yeah? (Foul language blurted.) *Go ahead, you couldn't last a week in my world!*

I was trying to have fun with my kids. I knew they had cabin fever and were bored. But it was too late and I had gotten up too early. I never actually had a chance to catch my breath. I smiled here and there, but it was forced. I had animated expressions, but they too were forced. I acted interested when my kids drew a scribble or when they built something high with their blocks … but I was faking it, 100%!

Today was one of those days that I just wanted to do over and it wasn't even over. I still had hours to go. Dinner … tubby-time … cleanup … and the usual bedtime struggles of getting them to stay in bed! Not until then would my day be done! Just the thought of how my day had started at 3:00 a.m. exhausted me. Today was a total waste. I did not get to talk to any of my friends. I did not get a chance to put on make-up, let alone comb my hair. I did not get 15 minutes where there wasn't a child needing me, or hanging on me.

Finally, after 18 solid hours-of-kids, they fell asleep. I had a chance to eat my first meal and visit with my sweetheart. We watched the news for a little while and it was the first time I really sat down for the day. The reporters rambled off a list of horrible things that occurred around the world. Two more families lost young boys serving in the military. Another mass grave was uncovered in some third world country, and locally two teenagers killed a woman while they were drag racing.

Wow. All of a sudden my world shrank. All of a sudden I wanted today to do all over again. The guilt suppressed any appetite I had. I put my plate down and went to the kids' room. They were crashed out. They were all cuddling up to their favorite stuffed animals. It was so tender and so innocent.

It's amazing to watch a sleeping child. And to think just hours earlier they were destroying everything in sight! Finally, I began to feel a calm come over me, the first time all day.

Then I felt guilty. I wished I had today to do over. Not to do again, but to erase. Erase the way I acted. I wanted to banish *grouchy me* from my children's minds. I was impatient and ungrateful. How could I have wished for my old life back?

I felt ashamed especially knowing that right now another family is probably notifying loved ones that their child had been killed. Right now there are children confused and scared because their mother had been in a fatal car accident.

All of a sudden I felt like I failed my children, at least today. I wanted it back. It was a long day, yes. But if I knew this morning what I know now I'm certain that I would have handled situations differently.

Looking at their tiny, seemingly innocent little faces I wondered what it was they were dreaming about.

The Mother who was killed in the drag-racing accident was on her way home from the grocery store. In fact, we lived in the same neighborhood. We shopped at the same grocery store. I'm sure this Mom was just like me and *assumed that she had another day to do the same thing over again.*

I feel like I short-changed my kids. Like I robbed them of a happy day with their Mommy. I know I am probably being too hard on myself, because the kids really cranked it up loud today! But really, what if today had ended differently? What if today ended like someone else's day? What if my baby was snatched out of my arms, never to be seen again?

Today is done and I admit it will be hard to fall asleep

tonight. I am racked with *Mom-guilt*. All I can do now is kiss my babies and whisper to each of them *I love you*. The other thing I can do is thank God for granting me another day, another day to do it all over again. Pee accidents, or not.

The following day I came across a picture I had taken of my kids. In it they were sound asleep and holding hands. I framed it and hung it on a wall that I walk by all day long. I've made it my new reminder that no matter how bad my day is bound to get … it will always end like this.

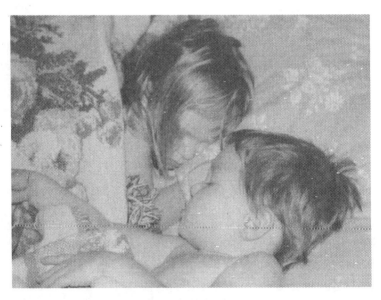

On hard days, I remember how it's going to end.
Scotty & Amanda

Full Moon Rising

Last night there was a big full moon and not a cloud in the sky. Jeff and the kids were playing together in the living room, so I grabbed my coat and snuck outside for a while. Full moons have special meaning to our family and so when I see one I try to appreciate it, if only for a few minutes.

It was wintertime and there was some snow on the ground. The neighborhood was quiet and Christmas lights decorated the streets. As I stood under the millions of stars I couldn't help but first think about my mom and how much I loved her. I thought about my kids and my husband and all the other wonderful people in my life who loved me as much as I loved them. I took in the magnitude of it all. I hoped my mom had seen the moon too. I just kept looking towards the sky, appreciating everything. To myself I thought, *I have such a beautiful life.* It seemed hard to imagine that there was a time where I dreaded, even hated, the holidays. It seemed hard to imagine that there was once a time in my life where I felt more pain, than peace. It's hard to believe now, because that place in my mind is worlds away.

My parents divorced when I was in my early 20's. It was ugly … it was messy … and it was heartbreaking. Our family crumbled into a million pieces. Not one of us were immune to the grief. My siblings and I started going our separate ways, shutting down our emotions and depending on our friends, rather than on each other. In a vain attempt to escape the pain, each of us began making what we thought were easy-out life choices, but in the end were the kind of decisions that were destructive to our own health and spirituality. But the heartache and sadness of our parents' separation had overwhelmed us and we lost our way. Life wasn't as important anymore and in one way or another we started giving up on goals and dreams, love and basic everyday happiness. It felt like they had betrayed us.

Like all families, we had been through many ups and many downs, but we had always done them together. After surviving more than twenty years of marriage, only then to divorce made little sense at the time. At least it did to us. Still, they followed through with it despite the outrageous and outspoken things we said, or did.

Some of our wild behaviors gained momentum. The family get-togethers were more explosive than they were comforting. Blame, anger and frustration became the new favorite topics of conversation. No one had the magic pill to change things back to the way they had been, though we gave that a try too.

A few years passed, and still our family was unable to shake the side effects from our parent's divorce. It was killing my mom that her children felt so miserable. It was obvious we were not close like we used to be. Christmas definitely stirred up the most hurt and was a particularly sensitive time for all of us. The nostalgia of the holiday season became a horrible reminder of what we no longer had.

So, back to last night. Here I was on my porch looking up at the sky, alone. It's December, but more significantly, it is the holiday season. My life now does not compare to those gut-wrenching memories of Christmas past. Today my emotions overflow with appreciation for my life and best of all I feel peaceful. In the end, our family's tragic end found a new beginning after all. It wasn't easy and it wasn't overnight. But it was worth it.

The healing really began with our mother. She started asking us to watch out for the full moons. She wanted us to know that wherever we happened to be in the world, all we needed to do was look up to the moon and know she was thinking of us. *The moon would be our compass to her love.* Full moons were meant to be special reminders. Those first couple of years she would call, or leave messages and say, "There is a full moon outside. I'm looking at it right now and thinking of you. I love you." And she was consistent. She called every time there was a full moon! Sure enough, over time the moon has become our symbol, the compass of our mother's love. In fact, more often then not, we are the ones now to call and remind one another of a full moon.

It's true that I have had some impossible things placed in my lap. And there have been times where the pain seemed insurmountable. But it is also true that I have never stopped trying. I have never stopped putting one foot in front of the other. Sure there were times I wanted to give up, but I never did … and here I am.

It is scary raising children. Your mistakes can cause your babies to hurt inside and even cry. I am a parent, but I am also human. I still struggle with self-esteem and I still have bouts of feeling sorry for myself. Sometimes I do not live up to my full potential and sometimes I wished I had done things differently. But then I snap out of it and remember that I am a Mom. And I remember that I have purpose in the world.

Last night as I admired the moon, I thought of my children. I know my babies are going to have many, many heartbreaks in their life and I very well may be the cause of some of them. It's tough being a parent. There is so much responsibility. But it is also true that I have the integrity and common sense to teach my children how to survive in this world. I am committed to my family the way my mother is committed to ours. It's entirely possible for me to introduce my children to a world of hope and opportunity, so long as I arm them with a strong spiritual foundation. By doing so, my children will always be able to find their way home.

Maybe my mom did fail in her marriage, or maybe her marriage failed her. That does not matter to me anymore. What matters to me is that she did not stop putting one foot in front of the other. Failing is not about making mistakes. It's about giving up! My mother's world came crashing down around her years ago and our broken hearts shattered along with it. It wasn't the fuzzy-warm story about the moon that saved us. It was her willingness to keep trying, coupled with her devotion and steadfastness that mattered most of all.

So, last night as I looked at the moon, automatically I thought of her. I compared the love I have for my own children against the size of the universe, needless to say that paled in comparison. I could hear my babies inside giggling with their daddy; I couldn't help but smile and appreciate that I really do have the most wonderful life. With that I said goodnight to the moon, and went back inside to play with my family.

Amanda & Daddy leaving treats under the tree Christmas Eve 2002. Unfortunately, in the end all that was left for Santa were milk and wrappers!

Oh, the Memories

Jeff and I had ten years together before children became part of our history. Yet, rarely today do we pick a memory to reminisce about that does not include the last four years. The biggest smiles we get come from talking about our kids. To describe our life now is like saying, *"We missed our flight, the hotel lost our reservation and my purse got stolen! But it was the best vacation ever!"*

As parents, we are in this stuff day in and day out so we do not think we are ever going to forget. When our baby is crying and we want them to stop, we think, *There is no way I am ever going to forget that sound.* But we do. When our children are learning to talk we think, *That gentle toddler voice is so cute, I am never going to forget their mismatched words.* But you do. And when our kids say something sweet or do something funny we instinctively think, *I'm always going to remember that!* But we don't. I hate to imagine all the cute stories I've lost because I assumed that surely, I would never forget.

In an effort to document my family's history, I want to share with you some of the favorite things I do remember. Besides, what kind of Mother would I be if I passed up another chance to brag about my family? These are just little tidbits and short stories that hopefully will have you smiling. There is no particular order and the overall message might simply be to honor the gift that children give, *the gift of laughter*.

~ It was the summer of 1999. Jeff and I were in the car headed to our favorite Mexican restaurant for dinner. We did not have any children at the time. I'd always been a terrible cook and as a result I never had anything in the cupboards to eat, *not ever*. That was frustrating to Jeff. So, on the way to the restaurant I said, "Honey some day when we have kids, I promise I will learn how to cook."

Three weeks later I found out I was pregnant. Immediately, Jeff reminded me of the promise I had made just weeks earlier. Had I known then what I know now, perhaps I would have chosen my words a little more carefully.

To this day cooking is not my strong point, but under the circumstances I have little choice. Besides, no restaurant in their right mind would allow our family through the door! No place that I would eat at anyway.

~ I am not a person who particularly likes to be pregnant. All I seem to do is eat and cry, cry and eat. During one of my pregnancies I was doing just that ... eating. It was the middle of the night and I was head first into a gallon of ice cream. Leaning on the counter with the microwave door propped open, I was reading my gossip magazine against its light. Because I was so tired I kept stumbling all over the place. I had even muttered to myself, "I wish this ice cream wasn't so good, because I am really tired!" Rather than going back to bed, I wedged my big belly into the corner and kept pigging out! Unable to stand still, I gave up and went back to bed. Turns out I really was tired. The next morning I learned that I as I stood there, I had been oblivious to the fact that I'd eaten *straight through a 6.0 earthquake.*

~ It was September 26, 2002. I was pregnant with Lindsay and had gotten up to pee (for the hundredth time). Before climbing back into bed I checked on the kids, when something happened that I'll never, ever forget. For the second time in my life, to my recollection, I saw an Angel. That's right, *an Angel.* The room was pitch black except for this image which was hovering over my daughter. We spoke to one another through our minds and she told me that she was my daughter's Guardian Angel. Her face was beautiful. She had long golden blonde hair and appeared to be in her 30's. What surprised me most was that she had massive, feathered wings. I know that Angels are often depicted this way, but I never really believed they did have wings. But this one did. We spoke a while, I thanked her for loving my child as much as I did. Then her light shrank into a small ball and disappeared, though I still felt her presence there.

The next day I was playing outside with my kids and noticed a feather on the ground near my feet. I picked it up and gave it to my daughter. I told her what I saw the night before and that her Angel wanted her to have this feather. She just said, "Oh cool. Thanks, Angel!"

To this day, we find all kinds of feathers and we find them everywhere! We find them around the house, in the car and even during the wintertime. Once I was curling my hair in the bathroom and a feather floated down just out of the blue.

~ My son was serving a *time-out*. When it was done I said, "Okay, honey, you can come out now. Are you going to be a good boy and stop eating the play dough?"

He replied with conviction, "Nope, not yet Mommy. I like it." And back in the room he went.

~ My daughter, Amanda, was doing her very best to make sure I had a particularly frustrating day. In the process of losing my mind, I scolded her, and lowered my parenting standards to name-calling. I said, "Amanda, you are making me crazy! You're being a real stinkerbutt!"

She yelled back, "I'm not a stinkerbutt, Mommy! I'm Princess Stinkerbutt!" Then she demanded of me, "Say it, Mommy! Say I'm Princess Stinkerbutt!"

Because she would not let up, *Princess Stinkerbutt* got her wish, and in the end we were both laughing. She taught me a good lesson too. Name calling only leads to more trouble.

~ I was changing my clothes and Amanda was in the room, too. Apparently she was paying too close attention because she said, "Look Mommy, you have a tummy like Daddy's. And Daddy has boobs like you!"

I just replied, "I know, honey, and its all your fault."

~ My son wanted ice cream, but I told him he had to finish his watermelon first. He said, "I did!"

With that, Amanda handed me her lunch plate with leftover rinds saying, "Me too, Mommy. I want ice cream!"

Naturally with that I said, "See, Scotty, Amanda is getting ice cream. She finished her watermelon."

Just then my daughter corrected me, "He ate his watermelon."

"Where is it then?" I asked.

She pointed to his plate and said, "Look, right there. He ate it!"

Sure enough he had ... rind and all! I guess I had been *too specific* with him. He got his ice cream after all.

~ After experiencing one too many kid tantrums, I stopped taking them in public all together (not counting kid places). It was not worth the embarrassment. But after a while I let my guard down and broke my own rule. Amanda had been a good girl all day, so as a reward I let her go to the grocery store with me. My husband questioned my judgment, but I said, "It will be okay, I only need a few things anyway." And it was. Until we hit the check out line.

There was an elderly man in line next to us who was cracking these long farts, oblivious that anyone could hear him. Until after about the third time. Having been polite long enough, Amanda said as loud as she could, while holding her nose… "Eeww! It stinks in here! Can't you hear him farting, Mommy? Tell him to stop!"

~ Jeff was unloading the dishwasher. My son said, "Daddy what are you doing? That's Mommy's job."

~ A few months ago, Amanda had a doctor's appointment for her immunization shots. Apparently she'd been on quite a growing spurt, though I did not realize how *spurty* it was until I the moment I cleaned her up to leave.

Everything in her closet was way too small. To make matters worse, anything that might have worked sat mangled in the laundry basket waiting to be folded. I could not even cram her toes into her shoes though I tried. I had to be there in the next twenty minutes! I was panicked. How could I have done this to my child? Where had my brain been the last month?

Amanda is a fashion goddess. She constantly changes from one princess outfit to another, ten times a day or more! She may have a shortage in regular clothing, but she does not have a shortage in silky, lacey, fluffy princess dresses. She has scads of plastic high heels, hats, scarves and fashion accessories to complete any ensemble. When I say she likes fashion, I am not exaggerating … her panties even have to coordinate! She can throw an outfit together that would seem outlandish to the average person, but miraculously she pulls it off like the next Versache!

So I plain did not notice that she did not have any *regular* clothes to wear! Honestly, I didn't have a single thing to put on her. I felt like a really lame Mom. I sat next to her brainstorming, when suddenly she said, "Mommy, can we go now?" With the sound of her sweet little voice I realized *she's just three!* Three year-olds are learning how to dress themselves. Everyone knows that, especially doctors! Super Mommy to the rescue! Suddenly I sat up, and with excitement in my voice I proudly announced, "Honey, go pick out your favorite outfit … we're going bye-bye!"

Moments later she was good to go … tap shoes, blue Cinderella gown, elbow length satin gloves and of course carrying her wand so she'd be ready to bestow wishes as needed. Turns out my little tiara bedecked princess was the hit of the hospital! Doctors and patients alike stopped in their tracks just so they could say hello! I was saved and she was thrilled!

We went shopping the very next day. That's never going to happen again on my watch.

~ A friend had given me a bouquet of fresh flowers. Wanting to enjoy them, I placed them in a vase and set them on the kitchen table. A while later all the flowers had been plucked off. Mad of course, I demanded to know, "Who did this?"

Amanda tattled, "Sammy did it, Mommy."

Sammy is the cat.

~ My son was crying and I could tell something was wrong. It was the *hurt* cry.

I said, "Honey, are you okay? What happened?"

With tears streaming down his face he said, "My poop is stuck Mommy. Can you get it?"

~ Jeff and I were watching cartoons with the kids. A while later we noticed they had left, but we were still watching their show. We changed the channel and laughed. Just then Amanda came back in the room scolding us, "What the hell is going on in here?"

Oops. We looked at each other embarrassed and said, "We've heard that before."

~ I had taken my kids to church for the first time. During the services they prayed, of course. Confused, one of my children shouted, "Look, Mommy, he's sleeping!"

The other little darling responded, "Shhhh... it's naptime."

After that, I began teaching my children to pray. Together we recite a poem and then say our *Thank you for* .... My son finally caught on, and now proudly does them on his own. This was his just a few weeks ago:

"Now I lay me down to sleep, I pray the Lord my soul to keep. May Angels watch me through the night, until I wake at mornings' light. Thank-you for Puppy, batman cape and boobs. Amen."

A Friendship Thank You

Womanhood is a lovely process of physical beauty, maturity, independence and the confidence in yourself to obtain all of that. How we decide what is important or beautiful is up to us, and us alone. Realizing this is not only personal, it is empowering. Womanhood is not achieved at puberty or on our wedding day, but throughout our lifetime.

A female's ability to listen, hear, be intuitive and compassionate are instinctive. If these traits are nurtured we will discover our true potential and life's purpose. It is the education of mistakes, the way we handle challenging and difficult circumstances that add personality, opinions and even humor to our character. We all have a destiny.

Unfortunately, many of us are more comfortable with chaos, stress, and sadness. What I have learned about constantly living in a state of trauma and drama, blame and anger is that the only life you will succeed in accomplishing, is a lonely one. Too many of us refuse to rise up and find the courage it takes to overcome our personal failures. Too often we refuse to rise above tragedies caused by our own choices. And too often we refuse to rise above situations we have no control over; situations forced upon us. Please hear me when I say this

… choosing to give up is not only detrimental to yourself, but also to your loved ones. No matter your situation, no matter your age, there is never an appropriate time to give in and give up. We will always have control of our own destiny!

When your life seems overwhelming, it is only because somewhere, sometime you gave away so much of yourself that you got lost. Whatever in your life is unsettling, whatever in your life is not happy, know this: Your partner did not take it, your kids did not take it, your job did not take it. Somewhere along the way you gave something else more attention, more care, more priority than you gave yourself. The consequences cannot help but leave you feeling trapped.

It's true some women may have financial privileges, some may have been blessed with exquisite looks and some may be exceptionally smart. That is great. The Universe has gifted all of us with something, something useful and beautiful.

So why is it as women, we are famous for *diseasing* our own self-esteem? Imperfect figures, failed relationships, broke, homely … who cares? Each of those things can be changed, given the desire. They are all fixable. If you do not desire it, then it must not matter. Does it?

So answer me this. What is your talent? What is your best trait? What is *your plus*? Name one. Terrific! Consider it obtained. If YOU think it is good, if YOU think you have *it*, then YOU MUST!

If the answer you gave includes someone else, or you cannot think of anything at all, then I have no doubt you feel lost. This is a dangerous state of mind. If you consider your life unproductive, unfulfilled or unhappy then you most certainly have veered off course from your destiny and your life's purpose.

The moments in life that you embrace, agree to challenge, to grow and to risk are the moments you become the woman you were designed to be. Maybe there is such a thing as a Lady who can "do it all." If there is such a Lady, I have neither met her nor heard of her. I personally believe that no matter the circumstances, every single one of us is capable of fantastic feats and capable of stunning accomplishments.

Women are a combination of people whom we admire. To me, this is why it makes sense that our seemingly insignificant choices and achievements are so valuable. Maybe a woman's lack of self-worth tends to get the attention. But I know better. All women are treasures to this Universe!

We have the tremendous ability to listen and hear at the same time.

We are instinctively compassionate.

We are automatically giving and considerate on every level.

Women are tolerant, women are patient and women are forgiving.

Women are *the* definition and very expression of LOVE.

It is my experience that when I behave in a manner that is *true to myself,* I accomplish the most. I do not mean to imply that being true to myself comes with ease. Not at all. Being true to myself usually heads me directly on the path straight towards some of my most difficult experiences. However, in the end they are experiences that have reinforced my self-esteem. They are challenges that taught me what I was really capable of and because I learned from them I neither regret them nor do I feel ashamed by them.

I love my life and I like myself. My weight fluctuates and I am not as beautiful as I was a few years ago, but I am comfortable in my own skin. I am comfortable alone in my thoughts. I know my appearance glows and as my looks fade I depend on that even more. The times I am most in tune with my goals, and chasing after my desires, are the times a smile on my face seems automatic, and effortless. I also notice that good things tend to fall into my lap more often too.

Life energizes me when I am living in a manner that serves *my* life's purpose. I realize my posture is better, my goals feel attainable and maybe most important, the people I love most feel closer to me!

I know about trauma and drama because my mom used to be nothing but trauma and drama! I also know about selling yourself out because I have sold myself out. I have also flushed my self-worth down the toilet a few times too.

Then again, I also know about landing on your feet, because my mother landed on her feet. She landed on her feet against all odds, several times! I know about love and devotion, because of my mom. I know about patience and compassion, because of my mom. I know about forgiveness, because of my mom.

My mother continues to challenge herself. She makes everyday of her life matter! Through her example, I have learned that if she can do it, then why not me? If she allows herself to make mistakes, to forgive her own shortcomings, then I am allowed to also. If she is still taking care of her body, then I should be as respectful of mine. If she continues to create dreams and chase after them, well I must be able to do the same.

To all of you Moms out there, I hope you continue to share your talents. Please keep writing your poetry. Please keep painting, singing, sewing, running, cooking and schooling. Please keep practicing what it is you like to do, because you never know which one of us will need to step into your shoes, if only for a day. You never know which one of us Moms will inspire your child. And you never know which one of you Moms will be my child's inspiration!

If you always dreamed of parachuting, then do it! Do you secretly wish to be a ballerina, but don't have the ballerina frame? Who cares? Dance! If you always wanted a red convertible, then open a savings account and start saving for one! Giving life to our fantasies and desires lowers the stress level while setting a wonderful example for our family at the same time.

Please continue to share your stories. Share with us the funny ones, the sad ones and the goofy ones. It is the stories of benevolence, the stories of patience and forgiveness that teach me. I am not that young, but I am a young Mother with years of education ahead of me. I complain and get frustrated. Sometimes I feel overwhelmed with my responsibilities. There are so many things I need to learn in order to raise children who are confident, brave and defiant in the face of evil. I need to teach all of these things to my babies because someday they will not be babies anymore. Someday they are going to want to leave this safe place I have created. They are going to want to explore this dangerous world without me.

So to the Grandmothers, Foster Moms and Single Parents who carry the responsibility for those who would not, I thank you. Your courage, selflessness, and determination are truly commendable.

To the Moms out there who nurse and doctor my children, I thank you.

To all the Moms who lovingly care for your special needs child all the days of their life. Your dedication and devotion inspires me, and leaves me in awe of you.

To the Mothers who bravely protect your children from abusive husbands, predators and deadbeat-dads, thank you. Your stories give me courage to do the same and inspire my life.

To the Moms who make laws, enforce laws and create laws so that my family can have a safer existence, I thank you, too.

To the women who work minimum wage jobs, then go home and tend to your children, I do not appreciate how exhausting that must be! Despite the blisters on your feet and the aches and pains all over your body, you continue to put one foot in front of the other–because you love your family! That's especially inspiring to me.

To all the women who cared enough about my mother to share your insight, I thank you. You gave her the courage she desperately needed to battle through her darkest hours.

I thank each of you for stepping into this circle of friendship and for being part of this unspoken bond. While it may be the hardest thing in the world to do - *teaching our children to remain true to themselves*–it *is* the most important thing of all!

My mother is a wonderful person because she

continues to make her life matter. I am following in her footsteps; my sisters follow mine and our children follow ours.

Womanhood is a lovely process of physical beauty, maturity, independence and the confidence in yourself to obtain all of that. In honor of all the special ladies who are a part of me... I promise to always set goals and to dream beyond my wildest dreams.

I know I am more than just a Mom because like you, I am a gift to the world. Like I said at the very beginning of this journey–Happy Mother's Day to each of you ... whatever day today is!

An Encore

As I mentioned in the *Friendship Thank You* chapter, as women we are a combination of people whom we admire and whom we have met during our lifetime. I had the privilege to Nanny a wonderful little girl. I do not know whatever became of her family, as we lost touch over the years. But this little girl, along with her mother, gave me some of the best memories of my life. I had left a highly stressful working environment at the time I accepted this particular Nanny position. To this day I am grateful to this Mother for entrusting me with her child, because it was the best thing that could have ever happened to me.

Like children are known to do, this little girl touched my heart. She was full of spunk and sparkle! She opened my eyes into the many colors of her world. I was supposed to be caring for her, but really it was she who cared for me. Her company allowed me the chance to take a deep enough breath that my mind was able to calm and my heart could be heard. One of the very first nights as I put her to bed, she cupped her tiny little hand in mine. As I rocked her to sleep, there in the dark, I just thought to myself, *This child is so relaxed and she barely knows me. She must really be a happy little girl.*

The poem *The Wish Giver* was born during those wonderful times. Recently, I came across it and thought it ironic. So I decided to include this bedtime story for your babies to enjoy. You just never know what good things, good dreams can bring!

The Wish Giver

Do you know where wishes come from?
Do wishes come from the stars?
If so, who is in charge of all the star's wishes?
Is it the moon or the sun? Who is the Wish Giver?
Maybe the sun is the Wish Giver.
It is so bright and our sun can see all of the star's wishes.
On the other hand maybe the real Wish Giver would be the moon.
After all, everybody wants to land on the moon.
Or maybe the Wish Giver comes from the weather.
Yes, I think wishes must come from the clouds.
Clouds must grant the very best wishes!
Cloud 9.
Cloud 9 does mean the happiest cloud. That sounds right.
The Wish Giver is a wishing cloud!
And then the rain sprinkles down all the leftover wishes
called raindrop wishes.
You know ... the kind you catch in your mouth.
I think that sometimes the wind must send wishes too.
Only the wind puts its wishes on colorful floating leaves
and on those fluffy cotton-ball flowers.
Clever.
The Wish Giver is the weather!
But then again ... maybe it's not the weather.
I forgot about the Fairy God Mother.
Do wishes come from the Fairy God Mother?

I just want to know!
I want to know, who is Captain of the Wish Givers?
You're right ... you're right.
The Wish Giver has to be Santa Claus.
Oh, but what about the Easter Bunny, Cupid and the
Tooth Fairy?
This is all so confusing.
A single, simple, confusing question!
Okay ... Cupid is the Boss, since he runs our most important holiday,
Love Day.
But no, that cannot be.
A baby who bosses the Fairy God Mother?
That's not right. That sounds too silly.
Is the Tooth Fairy the Wish Giver?
That would make sense because the Tooth Fairy
is the richest of them all!
'Course, not all wishes are about money. Hmmm.
I am thinking. I am thinking about this hard.
What about the Easter Bunny?
Could the Wish Giver be the Easter Bunny?
Magic eggs, surprises, candy, hide and seek games.
That sounds like real wish giving to me!
But then again there is no way the Easter Bunny
could be the Wish Giver,
because the Easter Bunny's favorite thing
in the whole wide world are carrots.
Nobody in charge of wishes would choose vegetables over candy!
Hmmm.
I am back to thinking the Wish Giver must be Santa Claus.
Santa Claus does have a personal secretary, Mrs. Claus.
Santa Claus has a staff of employees; all the little elves.
Santa Claus and Rudolph too!

Yeah! I figured it out.
Santa Claus is the Wish-Giving Captain.
Santa Claus is in charge of our wishes.
Oh my goodness. You are right.
You do know where wishes come from ...
Wishes DO come from the heart!
Wishes come from your heart and wishes come from my heart.
Everybody has a heart.
Hearts even help you think of good wishes.
Hearts never take time off. They work day and night.
Hearts work on holidays, birthdays, school days and rainy days.
Hearts also work on ordinary days.
That's it. You are right! That's the perfect answer to my question.
Wishes come from the heart.
The heart tells the clouds, and the clouds go tell the stars.
Then the stars sprinkle your wishes over to the moon.
The moon that brings you sweet dreams,
Good night kisses and good night wishes.
The End.